The Adventures of Gogglz

Quest One: "A Whale of a Tale"

Story by Lori Callaghan

Lori Callaghan grew up in Rivers, Manitoba where she played outside with cardboard boxes, lawn chairs, and blankets under the summer sun and with sticks and shovels in the deep snow of winter. She moved to Alberta to pursue her dream of becoming a teacher and making a difference in the lives of children. She rose to the challenge of her profession: teaching, tutoring, and influencing over five hundred young minds and counting. Her dream to write a children's book percolated for years until this, her first published book. Lori is a dreamer and loves to think up new things. Lori lives in Carstairs, Alberta with her wonderful and crazy husband, Jeff, and three little adventurers: Reece, Keefer, and Kenedee. She enjoys traveling, being outdoors, spending time with family and friends, playing with her children, gardening, music, and writing.

Art by Rob Hall

Rob Hall is from the small town of Tottenham, Ontario. He has been residing in Calgary, Alberta since 1977 where he graduated from the Alberta College of Art and Design in 1994. Rob's talent spans over a variety of styles and subject matter, communicated through multiple media, including pencil, watercolor and acrylics. Rob is currently a freelance artist who enjoys traveling with friends, motorbikes, animals of all kinds and adventures with his dogs.

AnnBee Press Inc.

Printed and bound in Winnipeg, Manitoba, Canada by Kromar Printing Ltd.

AnnBee Press Inc.
www.annbeepress.com
www.gogglz.com

ISBN 978-0-97354011-6

Story by Lori Callaghan

Art by Rob Hall

Designed by Amy Beart
deep blue design

I wrote this book for

_____

*To my husband, Jeff, with whom every day is a grand adventure.
And to my babes, Reece, Keefer and Kenedee,
here's to many adventures together.*

~ Lori ~

*A special thank you to Brian Callaghan
who helped to bring Gogglz to life.*

3

Meet Gogglz.

gglz

R.HALL 04'

Gogglz loves to play
and use his imagination.

Building with
cardboard boxes
is his favorite
thing to do.

ROB. 05'

He is always gathering boxes...

from small boxes,

to shoe boxes,

even gigantic boxes!

One sunny afternoon,
while walking home from Grandma's house,
he exclaimed,

**"Today is a great day
for adventure and play."**

Finally at home,
Gogglz chose the perfect box
to become a sailing ship.

He tied on his handy tool belt filled with colorful paint brushes,

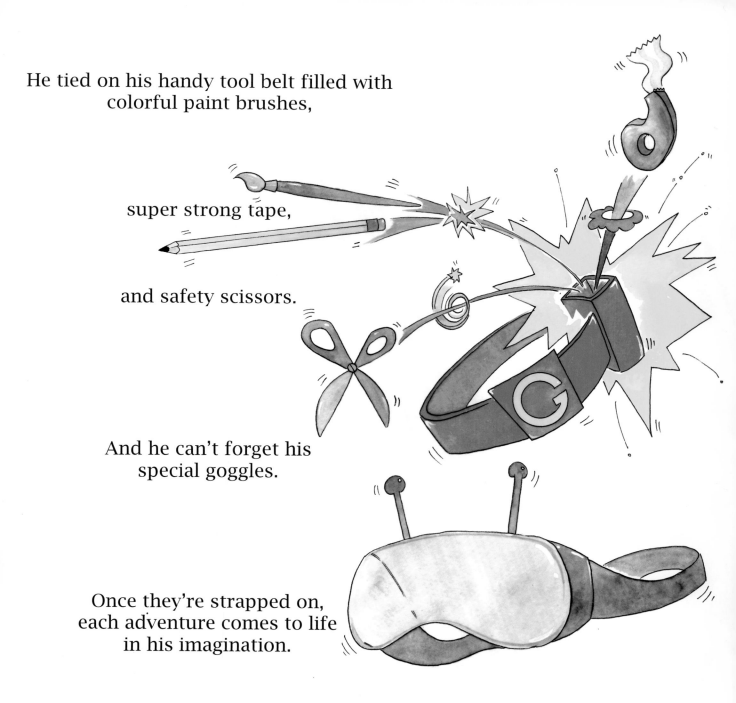

super strong tape,

and safety scissors.

And he can't forget his special goggles.

Once they're strapped on, each adventure comes to life in his imagination.

Gogglz was *finally* ready!

"Scissors cutting.

Paper folding.

My imagination
is exploding!"

BOOM!

"Snippity-snip.
I'm as busy as a bee,
with finally a ship to sail the sea!"
Gogglz shouted in great delight.

Gogglz proudly climbed aboard.

He braced himself for the final step.

And with a steady hand, he placed on his imagination goggles.

With a crash and a splash, he was sailing the ocean blue.

He must hold on tightly
because the waves are

big

and so are the sea creatures!

A big **whale** shark

was following Gogglz
looking very curious.

With a gust of wind,
the ship lost its sail.

Gogglz imagined a motor,
but it wouldn't go.

Then he tried paddles,
but they were too slow.

Gogglz *was in trouble!*

Suddenly the ship was sinking!

"Uh-oh!"
said Gogglz,
"I need to escape.
I forgot to use my
waterproof tape!"

He closed his eyes
and jumped off the ship,
only to land in the mouth
of the whale shark!

Shaking and staring,
Gogglz came face to face
with the enormous teeth.

18

He exclaimed,

"Your breath is so stinky,
but please Mr. Whale,
you don't want to eat me!"

Surprised, the whale shark
responded kindly,

"I won't eat you.
You've got it all wrong.

You see my tooth is very sore,
And I don't know what to do.

There's no dentist in these waters,
and I'm feeling really blue."

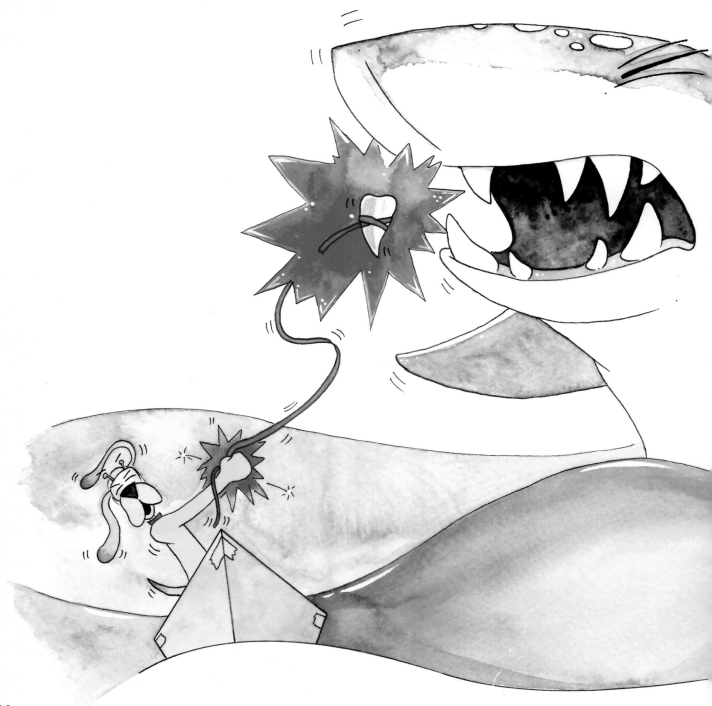

Gogglz breathed a sigh of relief.
He knew exactly how to help.

He took a piece of cardboard
from the sinking ship,
and using his imagination,
it was a rope instead.

He tied the rope to the sore tooth
and pulled with all of his might.

With a loud

POP

out came the problem.

The whale shark was so thankful.

He offered Gogglz a ride
back to dry land.

Upon reaching the shore,
Gogglz hugged his new friend.

He promised to come back and visit.

Gogglz learned two important lessons that day.

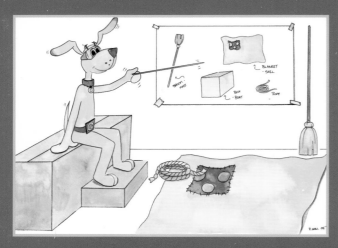

A grand adventure can be created
from *anything*
if you use a powerful part of you…

your imagination.

But more importantly,
Gogglz learned to look beyond
outside appearances
to see the *true value* of someone
on the **inside**.

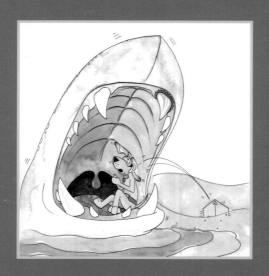